The Miracle Jar

A Hanukkah Story

by Audrey Penn
Illustrated by Lea Lyon

Tanglewood · Terre Haute, IN

To my beautiful cousins Erica and Ian who inspired this tale.

This book is also dedicated to those families who believe
in the ancient miracle of the lasting oil and
the greatest miracle of all: the fact that we are still sharing
the same story with our children and their children.
-AP

To Toni - LL

Published by Tanglewood Press, LLC, October 2008.

Text © Audrey Penn 2008.
Illustrations © Lea Lyon 2008.

Design by Amy Alick Perich.

Tanglewood Press, LLC
P. O. Box 3009
Terre Haute, IN 47803
www.tanglewoodbooks.com

Printed in China
10 9 8 7 6 5 4 3 2 1
ISBN 978-1-933718-16-3

Library of Congress Cataloging-in-Publication Data

Penn, Audrey, 1947-
  The Miracle Jar: a Hanukkah story / by Audrey Penn ; illustrated by Lea Lyon.
    p. cm.
  Summary: A family in the Old Country hopes to recreate the miracle of the first Hanukkah by making a
small jar of cooking oil last long enough to make a treat for each of the eight nights.
    ISBN 978-1-933718-16-3 (alk. paper)
  [1. Hanukkah--Fiction. 2. Hanukkah cookery--Fiction. 3. Jewish cookery--Fiction. 4. Jews--Fiction. 5.
Family life--Fiction.] I. Lyon, Lea, 1945- ill. II. Title.
  PZ7.P38448Mir 2008
  [E]--dc22
                                2008004769

Hanukkah came to a tiny snow-covered cottage in the Old Country. Eight-year-old Sophie awoke to the warmth of a crackling fire and the smell of hot buttered cinnamon toast.

"Tonight's Hanukkah!" she sang cheerfully as she danced out of her bedroom and into the glow of the fire. "When do we light the candles?"

"Just as soon as the sun goes down,"
Mother said with a smile and loving hug.
"But there's a lot to do before that."

Sophie finished her breakfast, ran to the cupboard, and removed the broom her father had made out of straw and wick. "I'll sweep the floors," she said, her face flushed with excitement. "That can be my Hanukkah present to you and Father!"

"That's a wonderful gift," applauded Mother. "We'll have a sparkling house for the holiday."

Sophie's younger brother Ruben shuffled out of his bedroom and
rubbed his tired eyes. "Is it Hanukkah yet?" he asked, yawning.

"Not until the sun goes down," Sophie told him. "But there's a lot to
do before that. I'm going to sweep the floors for my Hanukkah gift."

Ruben ate his breakfast and then sat at the table, looking thoughtful.
"What can I give as my Hanukkah gift?" he asked his mother.

"Well, let's see." Ruben's mother glanced around the house. Her eyes fell on the brass menorah her grandfather had made more than fifty years earlier. "You can polish the menorah," she told Ruben. "Then you can add the shamash and first candle for tonight."

Ruben grinned and went straight to work cleaning and shining the old menorah. When he was finished, he put the shamash candle in the center and the first night's candle on the end.

"It's beautiful!" said Mother. She picked up Ruben and twirled him around the room. "This will be the nicest Hanukkah ever."

Before long, Father appeared in the kitchen doorway, carrying an armload of firewood. He shook off the freshly fallen snow and greeted his family. "My, my, my. The house is so nice and clean. And the menorah shines like a bright new sheckel. I wonder, who did such a beautiful job?"

Sophie and Ruben jumped up and down. "Those are our Hanukkah gifts to you and Mother!" Sophie told him excitedly. "I swept the floors, and Ruben shined the menorah!"

"Those are the best gifts we have ever received," said Father. "Thank you. And we're all looking forward to your holiday treats," he told Mother.

"Well," Mother said thoughtfully, "If we're going to have my holiday treats, we're going to need an eight-day miracle, just like the first Hanukkah miracle."

"The first Hanukkah miracle?" asked Ruben.

Father smiled as he took off his coat and boots,
then gathered his children around the fireplace.

"The miracle your mother is talking about has to do with the sacred oil that stays lit above the Torahs in our temple.

"You see, in ancient times, when Judah the Maccabee and his followers reclaimed their temple from the Syrian king, they cleaned it and prepared it for rededication. The word 'Hanukkah' means rededication.

"But when the sacred temple menorah was relit, there was only enough oil to burn for one day. It's supposed to remain lit at all times. Back then, it took eight days to make a new supply of sacred oil, which meant there wouldn't be enough oil to keep the menorah lit while more was prepared. Then . . . the most amazing thing happened."

"What?" asked Ruben.

"A miracle!" rejoiced Father. "That single day's worth of sacred oil lasted eight whole days and nights, keeping the menorah lit while more purified oil was made. That's why we light eight candles. It's to celebrate the miracle. The shamash represents the tiny bit of oil that stayed lit."

"Are you going to make a supply of oil as your gift?" Sophie asked her mother.

"No, dear. But I am hoping for a similar miracle. There's only a little bit of cooking oil in the cabinet, and we need oil to make our eight holiday treats. I'm not sure there's enough oil to last all eight days of Hanukkah." Mother reached up and pulled the jar of oil down off the shelf and showed it to everyone. "The jar is almost empty, and there's too much snow on the ground to go fetch more from the store."

Sophie clapped her hands excitedly. "Then that will be our family gift. We'll make the oil in the jar last all eight nights of Hanukkah and make our own miracle."

"What a wonderful idea!" agreed Father. He made a label that read "Miracle Jar" and tied it to the glass container using a string. "Let's see if our Miracle Jar will surprise us like the sacred oil surprised Judah the Maccabee."

That night when the sun went down, Father stood before the brass menorah and sang a prayer. He then took a small stick from the fireplace and lit the shamash. The tiny light sent a dancing glow onto the mantle and ceiling. Sophie and Ruben took hold of the shamash and together lit the first Hanukkah candle.

When they returned the shamash to its place on the menorah, they welcomed Hanukkah with a song and a spin of their dreidel. Father called Sophie and Ruben over to his chair and handed each a shiny gold coin called gelt. "These coins are to remind us that after Maccabee became an independent state, they proudly minted their own coins instead of using those of the Syrians."

"Well, I suppose it's time for our first miracle gift," announced Mother. She led Sophie to the kitchen where together they peeled and grated three large baking potatoes. When they finished, Mother opened the Miracle Jar and poured some of the oil into the heavy black skillet. When the oil was nice and hot, she poured the potato batter into four little pancakes. She and Sophie watched as the latkes bubbled and fried, turning a nice, crispy golden brown. When they cooled, Sophie, Ruben, Mother, and Father each delighted in a potato pancake. They all agreed that it was a very tasty holiday gift.

When the remainder of the oil cooled, Sophie's mother poured it back into the special jar, to be used for the remaining treats.

On the second night of Hanukkah, Sophie and Ruben lit the shamash and two candles.

After a game of dreidel, Mother opened the Miracle Jar and poured the oil into her black skillet. When the oil was piping hot, she dropped small hand-rolled doughnuts into the pan. Soon they sizzled to a delicate brown.

Mother placed the doughnuts on a plate to cool, filled each one with jelly, then sprinkled them with a flurry of snow-white sugar. Everyone laughed at Ruben's white powder mustache.

The third night of Hanukkah brought
fried corn fritters to the table.

And on the fourth night, Mother made
Sophie's favorite treat: crispy, crunchy,
fried potato sticks with salt and butter
on the side.

The fifth night of Hanukkah brought fried bread and powdered sugar to the table.

But Sophie could see that the oil in the Miracle Jar was dwindling, and she wondered if all eight nights would bear gifts.

Sophie and Ruben lit three candles each on the sixth night. They sang songs and watched the candles slowly melt away as they ate thinly sliced apples that had sizzled and softened in the oil-coated pan.

"I can't believe it's already the seventh night of Hanukkah," said Mother after the candles were lit and the songs were sung. "But I'm not sure we're going to have our special miracle." She opened the Miracle Jar and turned it upside down. The last drops of oil danced across the hot black skillet. Sophie and Ruben sprinkled peanuts onto the oil and laughed as the peanuts popped and twirled, turning a crisp, crunchy brown. But there was no oil left to pour back into the jar.

"I guess we can't make our last holiday treat," said Sophie, sounding very disappointed.

"Well, that's the amazing thing about miracles," said Father. "They always show up at the most unexpected times. Let's see what tomorrow night brings."

Father was right. When the last night of Hanukkah began, and the shamash and eight holiday candles were lit, it was hard to feel sad in the glow of the shimmering menorah. "Maybe we can have another Miracle Jar next year," said Sophie. "Then we can have eight miracles instead of just seven."

"Remember what Father said. Sometimes, all it takes is a little imagination to come up with a Hanukkah miracle."

Mother led her family into the kitchen, then reached up and took the empty Miracle Jar off the shelf. Next, she opened the door to the pantry and reached up to the top shelf. Her fingers knew just where to go as she grabbed hold of a small piece of cheesecloth.

While her family watched, Mother stuffed the cloth inside the jar and wiped the jar's oil-coated sides until they were sparkling clean. She then took the cloth and spread the oil on the bottom of her skillet. There was just enough oil to coat the pan.

As the oil heated, Mother whipped up a batter made from flour, water, and an egg and poured it into the skillet. When the large fried pancake was ready, she turned the skillet upside-down and dropped the hot treat onto a towel. Father and Ruben peeled and mashed an apple, and then Sophie added a stream of sweet golden honey.

When the mash was ready, Mother spread it onto the pancake, rolled it into a log, and sliced it into four equal parts. Everyone got a piece of the eighth miracle treat.

Sophie was very excited. She hugged her mother, then licked her fingers clean of the apple and honey. "You did it!" she told her mother. "You made a real Hanukkah miracle! You made the oil last all eight nights, just like the oil in the temple!"

Father was also very excited. "Now we know how surprised everyone must have felt on that very first Hanukkah," he told his children. "Isn't it nice to know that some of the nicest gifts are the ones that surprise us the most."

Sophie and Ruben watched as the shamash and the last eight candles melted away.

"Happy Hanukkah," Sophie told her family when the last of the flickering flames went out.

"Happy Hanukkah," echoed Ruben as he licked the last of his honey-coated fingertips.